Deadly Night

F. A. Witte

Published by F.A. Witte, 2024.

This is a work of fiction. Similarities to real people, places, or events are entirely coincidental.

DEADLY NIGHT

First edition. October 31, 2024.

Copyright © 2024 F. A. Witte.

ISBN: 979-8224350131

Written by F. A. Witte.

To all my Halloween fans, this one is for you.

Prologue

I sat with my sister Mylah in front of a fire station. It was Halloween night. Our mother was supposed to take us out trick or treating but instead she wanted to go to a party with her boyfriend. She handed us a blanket because she forgot our jackets at home.

"Wait here and I will be back as soon as possible." She said to us.

"Are we still going to go get candy?" My baby sister Mylah asked.

"As soon as I get back. I promise." Another broken promise out of her mouth.

Mylah was too young to understand that our mother was a compulsive liar. I sat there quietly because I knew what she was doing.

It felt like hours had gone by, but I didn't have a good judgement on time then. I just knew it was getting colder by the minute.

"When is mom coming back?" Mylah asked in a soft voice.

"Soon," I lied to her. I knew our mother wasn't coming back for us. She left us here for a reason. She didn't want us anymore. I knew Mylah's heart would be shattered so I wanted to protect her. One day she will understand but right now there was no point in explaining it to her.

"What are you two doing sitting out here?" A deep voice from behind us spoke.

We both turned around to see who it was. A tall bulky man in a firefighter uniform stood over us.

"We are waiting for our mom." I started to whimper.

"Why don't we go inside and wait for her. It's warmer in there and I believe I have some potato soup you both would love."

Mylah looked at me confused. "What is potato soup?"

"It's food," I answered. I jumped up from the curb and grabbed my sister's hand and followed the man into the station.

Chapter One

Present Time

"You are breathtaking." I heard someone say with an accent.

I looked up from the book I was reading to see who he was. I raised an eyebrow in amazement by what I saw in front of me. His plain white shirt hugged his muscles tightly. He was in shape for sure. He had the sexiest jaw line I had ever seen. Almost like he was created right out of my dreams. He didn't look familiar. There was no way he was talking to me. I glanced behind me just in case he was talking to someone else. That's happened to me before. I didn't want to relive that embarrassment.

"Excuse me?" I replied to him not knowing for sure I heard him right.

"I said you are breathtaking." he repeated himself. "Do you come here a lot?"

I blushed as I set my book down on the table. "Thank you." I told him. "I actually do come here on a daily." I was flattered that someone as good looking as him would be interested in a girl that looked like me. Not that I'm bad looking or anything. He just looked like a model out of a magazine.

"Do you mind if I sit down with you?" he asked before pulling out the chair across from me. I nodded my head yes. He sat across from me and stared at me with his deep blue eyes. I started to feel awkward. I was sitting outside of my favorite diner 'Karla's' like I do every day at this time, reading the new book by James Patterson. My all-time favorite author. This has never happened to me before. I started to think this had to be a prank or something. I didn't want to look desperate or keep staring at him, but this man was gorgeous.

"Are you from around here?" I asked him to try to keep the conversation going. I didn't want to bore him.

"I'm from Australia originally but I've lived upstate for a couple of years now." he answered.

"That's cool. I could tell by your accent; you weren't from around here."

He grinned at me and licked his lips. I felt my face starting to heat up. "I happened to be walking by, and your beauty stopped me, and I just had to get to know you." his charm was on fire.

I've never experienced getting hit on like this. One for the books. I'll play his game. I was a little rusty in the field, but I'll try my best. "You are a sight to see yourself. Something right out of." I flirted back. His mahogany brown hair was pulled back into a man bun with an undercut underneath. From the look on his face, he was freshly shaved.

"Please tell me you're single?" he asked, placing his hands together like he was praying.

I chucked. "I am as a matter of fact but I'm not looking for a relationship." I was honest with him. Although I did imagine what fun we could have together.

DEADLY NIGHT 5

"You are too beautiful to be single." He went with a classic line. I wasn't impressed. He seemed more creative than that.

I chuckled. "If I had a penny for every time I've heard that line..."

"You'd be rich." He finished my sentence.

"Exactly." I smiled.

"Well, what if I told you I'm not like other guys." he smiled. I noticed a dimple on his left cheek but not his right. But that was one hell of a sexy smile he had.

"Yeah, I'd still be rich." I joked.

"Would you like a predate?" He leaned forward and smiled.

"What is a predate?" I asked curiously.

"I take you out, but it wouldn't be a date." he began to say. "It would be with a bunch of other people, so you can trust me. And you'll have the opportunity to get to know the real me in an environment that I enjoy."

"That sounds interesting." I've never heard of a predate before. I guess it couldn't hurt.

"So, what do you say?" he asked, being hopeful.

"I'll think about." I didn't want to just give in to him right away. Although I wanted to. This could be the beginning of something exciting.

"You don't even have to show up with me. And you can bring whoever you want." He tried to convince me.

His plan was working. I was curious about where he wanted to go. "Where am I supposed to be meeting you at?" I asked playing along

"There's this secret Halloween party tonight." he began to say before I cut him off.

"I don't do Halloween parties. Sorry." I was uninterested as soon as he said Halloween party. I hate scary stuff.

"Oh, come on it'll be fun. You don't even have to dress up." He tried to convince me again.

"I'm sorry. It's just not something I'm into." I explained. "This day isn't something I like to celebrate."

"If you change your mind, here is the address." He reached into the back pocket of his ripped jeans and pulled out a folded piece of paper. I grabbed the paper from his hand when he handed it to me. "I really hope you will come. I'd love to see you again."

I wanted to see him again too, but I knew that was unlikely. "I will see what I can do." I told him with no intentions of going or ever seeing this man again. He stood up from his seat and leaned towards me once again.

"The name is Arlo." he uttered then reached his hand out to me.

"Breigh." I grabbed his hand to shake it but instead he kissed it. I could feel the heat coming from my cheeks. He made me blush hard. The way he looked at me with those gorgeous eyes of his, it was hard to contain myself. I was already fantasizing what our children would look like. Hopefully more like him. For their sake.

"It was nice meeting you Breigh. I hope to see you tonight." he smiled.

"You too Arlo." I uttered as he walked away. I watched him until he disappeared with the crowd walking. There was no denying he was attractive.

"What just happened?" I said to myself out loud.

I unfolded the piece of paper he handed me and read it. It was a flyer for a Halloween party and haunted house in one.

Come party and get scared at the same time.
Located at 1211 N Archer Road
Look for the warehouse.

"That doesn't sound creepy at all." I said under my breath.

I folded the paper up how it was before and noticed Arlo printed his name and number on the back of it. Arlo Jones. Mrs. Breigh Jones. That had a ring to it. I giggled at how childish I was acting over a man I had just met. As much as I wanted to get to know him better, I knew I couldn't. I didn't need any distractions right now. Not while I'm still trying to find my sister Mylah. I glanced around at all the little kids in their costumes roaming the streets with their parents. Some were just adorable angels and pumpkins, and some were scary clowns and horror film characters. I imagined being a parent for a second. The thought quickly faded when I remembered I'm nowhere near qualified to be a parent.

Chapter Two

Mylah was twenty-two years old when she went missing. In fact, she went missing one year ago today. Halloween night. I remember our last night together like it was yesterday.

"Why don't you come to this party with me and Daegan?" she asked while she was getting ready in the bathroom. We shared an apartment together. I was sitting on the couch watching horror movies and eating popcorn. Even though I was terrified of scary films I often tortured myself watching them.

"No, I don't want to." I yelled to her not taking my eyes off the television

"Seriously Breigh. She peeked around the corner into the living room. "I really want you to meet my new boyfriend." she begged.

"I will in due time." I promised her as I took a handful of popcorn and shoved it in my mouth

"We've been together for six months now and you haven't even met him." she pouted.

"I said I will." I grew annoyed with her. "When the time is right, I will meet him."

"Do you promise Breigh? You say this every time we want to hang out with you." she pointed out.

"Mylah, stop please!" I shouted at her. "He isn't worth us arguing about."

DEADLY NIGHT

"He asked me to move in with him." she blurted out.

She now had my full attention. "Please tell me you told him no." I jumped up from the couch.

She didn't answer me. She just looked at me like she feared my reaction.

"You told him no right?" I asked again.

"I told him yes." she started to cry. She knew I would be upset with her actions. I had every right to be.

"Mylah what are you thinking? Why would you do that?" I questioned her. I wanted to know why she thought this was a good idea.

"Daegan loves me, Breigh You need to realize that." she tried to explain.

"He is just using you." I shouted at her.

"You don't know that. You have never even met him." She defended him. "He is a great guy, and he really does love me."

"I don't have to meet him to know he is no good for you." I shouted at her.

"Give him a chance Breigh." she begged.

"You are not moving in with him." I demanded her.

"I already have." she confessed.

"What?" I gasped. Those words cut me like a knife. I couldn't believe she would go behind my back and do something like this.

"You heard me." she said rudely. She has never disobeyed me before. This guy must have brainwashed her against me or something.

"Mylah, you didn't." I said in disbelief. I walked to her room and opened her door. It was empty except for the bed. I opened the drawers in her dresser, and they were all empty. I then went to her closet and opened it. Nothing. My heart was racing. I had never been so angry in my life.

"I told you." she said as she stood behind me. I was still in shock that my little sister moved out without me knowing about it. "We were going to tell you tonight during dinner and I had hoped you would have come out with us and celebrated me becoming an adult and making my first real adult decision. I love you Breigh, but I can't live with you forever."

"We made a promise to each other." I reminded her as I wiped the tears from my eyes before I faced her. The last thing I wanted was for her to know she made me cry

"When we were kids. We are not children anymore Breigh." she pointed out.

She was right. We weren't kids anymore. Our mother left us at a fire station when I was seven and Mylah four. We bounced around from family to family until I aged out of the system and got custody of my sister. I had to work really hard to get her and keep her. I knew little about our dad. He left us when Mylah was two. Shortly after he left our mother turned to drugs and men for closure. One of those men finally convinced her that we were too much baggage, so she didn't hesitate to let us go. Mylah doesn't remember every detail like I do. I still have nightmares of the last thing our mother said to me before she walked away.

"Take care of your sister for me. I'll find you both one day." She kissed both our foreheads and never looked back. I remember being cold and scared. I stayed strong for Mylah. That was sixteen years ago. Since then, I have busted my ass to take care of her. Lived with horrible strangers. The first few years I had high hopes that our mother would return. I finally gave up on the dreams when I was ten.

DEADLY NIGHT   11

    I knew I had to give in. I was scared to be alone but deep down I knew this day would eventually come. "You're right Mylah. You are absolutely right." I admitted. "You are no longer a child, and you deserve happiness in your life. Who am I to keep you from having that?" I had to let go of my little sister. She was a woman now and was able to make her own choices. Sometimes I felt she was still a kid, and I had to protect her but looking at her tonight she wasn't a kid anymore.

    "Oh Breigh," she wrapped her arms around my neck and squeezed me tightly. I hugged her back. I could tell she was crying happy tears.

    "You're messing up your makeup." I told her.

    "Oh, I'm not worried about that." she claimed. We let go of each other and both wiped our eyes.

    "I can't believe my little sister is grown up and moving out." I smiled at her. Even though it was breaking my heart for her to go. Who was going to keep me company in this apartment now? Being alone was my biggest fear. With Mylah leaving the nest I was going to be just that.

    "Daegan is a really great guy, Breigh. You are going to love him." She sounded like she was truly in love with him.

    "Well, I can tell you now, I already hate him. He's taking my sister from me." I teased her. Although deep down I did dislike him.

    "I won't be too far away, and I'll come hang out with you all the time." she promised.

    "I'm sure you would forget all about me in no time." I teased her.

    "I could never forget about you." she replied. "I have to go fix my make up now." she let out a light giggle.

I returned to the living room and let her finish getting ready. I wondered what life was going to be like without my sister so close to me. I'll get to see her maybe once a month. Yeah, sure she promised to come and see me all the time, but she doesn't realize being in a relationship is going to take up all her time. They'll have work and then one day kids. Where does that leave time for me? Holidays? I hate holidays.

Twenty minutes later she returned. "How do I look?" she spun around with a big smile on her face. Mylah looked stunning in her little black dress with a cross back and slit down the side. Her strapped around the ankle sandals complimented her legs nicely. Chandelier earrings hung from her ears, and they were the most alluring piece of jewelry I had ever seen.

"Wow." I said in amazement. "You look stunning."

"Thank you." she smiled.

"I thought you were going to a Halloween party not a fancy restaurant." I was confused that she wasn't wearing a costume.

"Well, we are going to a fancy restaurant before the Halloween party, but Daegan wanted me to dress nicely. Do you love the earrings?" she sounded giddy. It almost made me sick.

"I really do love them. Where did you get them?" I asked, not really caring about them.

"Daegan gave them to me for our sixth month anniversary." she said with a big smile plastered across her face.

"Looks like you picked a winner." I told her sarcastically. She didn't notice at all.

"Breigh, I have something else important to tell you." her voice turned to a serious tone.

"Don't tell me you two are already getting married or something?" I asked, hoping she would say no.

DEADLY NIGHT

"No, it's not that." she told me.

I gasped. "Are you pregnant?"

"No Breigh." she started to sound frustrated.

I was relieved that she wasn't. Although, it wouldn't be that bad having a little Mylah running around. "Then what is it?" what else could she possibly brag about?

"I wanted to tell you this sooner, but I didn't know how you would react." she hesitated to say.

"What is it, Mylah?" I was growing impatient.

"I found mom." she finally blurted out.

"We don't have a mom, Mylah." I chuckled. What in the world is she talking about?

"She's better now Breigh and she wants to meet you." she said to me.

"You've talked to her?" I gasped in disbelief. My heart fell from my chest and into my stomach. I felt betrayed.

"Yes, she has met Daegan already and she loves him. She is going to dinner with us tonight which is why I was really hoping you would come with us." she replied.

"I can't believe that you would betray me like that." I was furious with her. How could she after all I've done for her. This was worse news than her moving out. "After what that woman has put us through? How could you just welcome her with open arms? Do you not remember her walking away and leaving us there in the cold?" I reminded her.

"Breigh she was sick," she tried to make an excuse for her.

"She chose that lifestyle, and she chose that man over us. How could you be so forgiving?"

"She's changed." she had a shocked look on her face. "I thought..."

I didn't let her finish her sentence before cutting her off. "If you want her to be in your life then I want you out of mine." I screamed at her.

"You don't mean that." she began to cry.

Usually seeing her cry would make me feel bad for her but this time I was just so furious my blood was boiling. I was starting to sweat because of how upset I was. I wanted to hurt her. I had to restrain myself from hitting her. "Yes, I do. Now get out of my apartment." I demanded her.

Mylah didn't say a word to me. She grabbed her purse and keys off the table by the front door and walked out without saying goodbye. I was so furious with her. How could she give that woman any kind of attention after what she had done to us. She didn't love us. Now my own sister wants to let her back into her life. Did she forget I'm the one who has taken care of her all these years?

I took my anger out on the photos of me and Mylah that were hanging on my living room wall. The way I was feeling I didn't care if I ever saw Mylah again. I know she was young when our mother left us behind, so she didn't understand. The nerve of her thinking I would just welcome that woman back into my life with open arms. I would never give her the chance to hurt me again. She was going to hurt Mylah. I could feel it in my gut.

That was the last time I ever seen my sister. I regretted every word I said to her. Maybe if I was more open minded and could have controlled my anger better, she would still be here today. I've never heard anything else about our mother after Mylah disappeared. I didn't expect to ever hear from her anyways. Sometimes I would fantasize about a life with her in it. What it would be like to have a mom. A small part of me hoped she would have reached out to me but that was me just being stupid and letting my imagination take over me.

Chapter Three

I got back to my apartment around two in the afternoon. I threw my keys and purse on the small table next to the front door. I walked to my living room and threw myself down on the couch next to Layla Hankins who was already mid-through an under-budget horror film. Layla was Mylah's best friend. We became close after Mylah's disappearance. Layla became such a dark person after Mylah disappeared. She wore nothing but black and was constantly watching horror films and serial killer documentaries. I figured she was just having an identity crisis after Mylah was gone. They were usually attached to the hip. Layla hardly slept for six months trying to find Mylah. One day she just stopped and her whole aspect of life just changed. I know she misses my sister just as much as I do. That's why I believe she has changed so much. I can get her bubbly side to come out occasionally, but it is a job to do.

"Rough day?" she asked as she picked up the remote and hit pause. She was in her usual black attire. Black tank top with black sweats to match her pale skin. Her black eyeliner was extra heavy than usual, and I noticed she did a black touch up on her hair. Layla is a natural blond-haired girl, but she regularly dyes her hair black.

"It was interesting." I replied. I debated about telling her about Arlo. I wasn't in the mood to hear her all giddy. She always

DEADLY NIGHT 17

got overly excited when I met someone. She was convinced I needed a man in my life. Like that was going to fix me.

"What happened to make it so interesting?" she asked curiously.

Instead of replying to her, I pulled the flyer from my back pocket and handed it to her.

She opened it up and her face lit up. "We have to go!" she said overly excited.

I looked at her like she was ridiculous. "I'm not really interested in going." I admitted. "It's just not my scene."

"Who is this Arlo Jones guy?" she asked looking at the back of the paper. I wasn't sure how to explain him to her.

"It's the guy that gave me the flyer." I left out all the major details.

"Is he cute?"

Of course, that was the first question she was going to ask about him. "He is very attractive," I began to say.

Before I could finish, she already had him looked up on her phone. "Attractive is an understatement for him. He is a major hottie girl." she said as she scrolled through his photos.

"You really looked him up?" I playfully hit her with a pillow. I didn't even think to do that.

"Yes, on Instagram. He looks like a model." she pointed out. I leaned in closer to her so I could see what she was looking at. It was Arlo's profile. "You have to go if he's going to be there."

"I'm not going." I told her again. She needed to get that through her head. She wasn't going to convince me otherwise.

"Why not?" she asked. "This hot guy invites you and you just say no?" she said in disbelief.

"Any other day, maybe, but just not tonight." I told her. She knew what today was.

"You can't keep doing this to yourself Breigh." Her smile faded when she realized why I didn't want to go.

"I'm not doing anything to myself. I just really miss my sister." I explained. I stood up from the couch and walked to the kitchen. Layla followed behind me. I opened the fridge door and grabbed me a bottle of water. "Would you like one?" I offered her.

"No, what I would like is for you to get out of this apartment for once." she begged.

"I do get out. Everyday actually." I corrected her.

"To work and to read that's it." She wasn't satisfied with my answer.

"That's still getting out." I said sarcastically.

"Breigh, I know you miss your sister, and lord knows I miss her too. If she were here today, she would want us to go out and have fun." she made a point.

Mylah hated it when I acted like such a hermit. She always begged me to leave the apartment and do something other than work and read. She wanted me to meet new people and make friends, find a man to settle down with and start a family. Those weren't goals of mine. Those were her life goals. I didn't want kids or a husband or a white picket fence. I wanted freedom. I wanted to be alone lost in worlds of make believe. I wanted to be lost in books. My dream guy was always in the romance novels, and I wasn't dumb enough to know men in real life are nothing like the ones you read about. So why waste time looking for someone who doesn't really exist?

"It's just hard, you know." I hurried up and took a sip of my water before I started to cry. I could feel my eyes starting to water up talking about my sister.

"We can talk about her you know." Layla must have noticed I was about to cry. She looked like she was about to do the same.

"I know." I said as I put the cap back on the bottle and walked back towards the living room. It wasn't that I didn't want to talk about my sister. I just couldn't. I've had so much guilt built up over this past year because of my last words to her.

Layla followed me to the living room closely. "For Mylah. Please." she asked calmly. I stopped walking and turned to look at her. Her eyes were watery, and her face frowned. She knew those words would get me to cave. It wasn't the first time she had used them. I couldn't hold my tears back anymore.

"Fine!" I caved and was mad about it. Layla's face lit up as she jumped up and down with excitement while clapping her hands. I rolled my eyes at her. I think she just played me, and I fell for it. "I'm not wearing a stupid costume." I added.

"You don't have to." she said with a big smile on her face.

"Good. And if I say I want to leave then we have to leave." I told her.

"Deal." she said trying to hold in her excitement.

Chapter Four

Layla wore a black and purple corset with a Lolita tutu skirt. Fishnet stockings covered her legs, and she had the cutest lockdown knee-high boots. The gothic fashion wasn't my style, but she made it look sexy as hell. Her bangs covered half of her face, and she curled the bottom half of her hair. Black eye shadow and eyeliner covered her eyes, while a deep red matte lipstick covered her lips.

"Wow," I told her. "You are really rocking that style."

"Thank you. I always thought this outfit was too much but now is the time to try it out." she smiled as she twirled around in it. She stopped once she noticed what I had on. "Um, what is that?" she asked looking me up and down.

"What is what?" I asked confused.

"Breigh, what do you have on?" she asked horrified. I laughed at her. "I can't be seen with you dressed like that."

I guess my 'This is my costume' t-shirt and jeans weren't cutting it for her. "I told you that I wasn't wearing a costume." I reminded her. How did she forget so soon? I hope she didn't think I was just joking.

"It looks like you are an old boring lady. We are going to a party. You need to dress like you're young and fun, not some boring grandmother. No offense." she added.

"Geez, tell me how you really feel." I said sarcastically.

"Sorry, but no." she looked me down once more then returned to her room. After a couple of minutes, she returned with several outfits. "Try these on," she told me. "And hurry I don't want to be late." I didn't question her.

I grabbed the clothes from her and went to my room to try them on. After about twenty minutes I was starting to get frustrated. "Do you have anything other than black?" I yelled at her. She popped her head into my doorway.

"You know that I don't." she replied. She walked to my closet trying to see what she could find. She made disgusting faces as she moved the hangers looking through my wardrobe. "Where do you shop?" she asked. "The thrift stores?"

"Hey!" I was offended. I didn't see any problem with my choice of clothes. I wore what was comfortable for me.

"Sorry." she mumbled. "Hey what's in this box?" she asked as she found the box in the back of my closet. Before I could respond she already had the box pulled out of the closet.

"That's some of Mylah's things. Daegon dropped some of them off about seven months ago." I told her.

"You finally got to meet Daegan and didn't tell me about it?" she was shocked.

"Actually no, they were left in front of my door, so I assumed he was the one who brought them seeing how all her stuff was at his place." I explained. "I'm glad I didn't see him if I'm being honest."

"All he gave you was a box?" She tilted her head in confusion. "She had way more stuff than that."

"Yeah well, that's all that was left." I shrugged my shoulders. I was grateful that anything of Mylah's was left in the first place.

"Oh." she replied and continued opening the box.

"Do you still have contact with him?" I asked her curiously. I knew she had met him before. She was Mylah's best friend. She had to have met him before.

"Not in a while," she admitted. "The only thing that connected us was Mylah and since she's gone..." Layla paused and hid her face from me. I knew she was hiding her face to wipe a tear away. Talking about Mylah always made us cry but she was worth the slow torture. I missed my sister more than anything.

"He never reached out to me after she disappeared." I admitted.

"I'm sure he had his reasons," Layla mumbled as she pulled clothing out of the box.

"What do you mean by that?" I asked.

"Well," She looked at me before hesitating to speak.

"What do you mean by that Layla?" I asked again but this time I sounded demanding.

"Mylah didn't tell him a whole lot of good things about you." she finally admitted.

"What do you mean?" I asked, shocked. "I was always good to her."

"You were, but in her eyes, she seen it more as controlling."

"I can't believe she would say that about me!" I was upset and hurt.

"I'm sure she said it in anger. Daegan had the version of you that Mylah gave him, so he always kept his distance."

"But it isn't true!" I shouted.

"I know it's not true." she said to calm me down. "He doesn't know you like I know you and it doesn't matter anyways."

She was right. Why am I overreacting to a guy that I never met before? Who cares what he thinks about me? I know who I am. His opinion of me doesn't matter.

Layla pulled out a white blouse and admired it for a few seconds. Her face lit up. "I got the perfect outfit for you." she said as she stood up and ran out of the room with the blouse still in her hands.

I placed my face in my hands. I wasn't excited to see what she had come up with. Our fashion tastes were completely different. Whatever it was, I knew I wasn't getting out of wearing it.

Chapter Five

"I look like a pirate." I complained. Layla put me in a pearl white silk blouse with some black Palazzo pants. I felt like I was dressed for a business meeting more than I was for a Halloween party.

"It's better than what you had on before." she said as she searched for a parking spot in front of the crowded warehouse. It was weird that this place was in the middle of nowhere. Who puts a warehouse in the middle of nowhere? Corn fields covered the whole back of the building and went on for miles. I could feel the vibration of the music from sitting in the car. I knew it was going to be really loud once we were in there. I felt bad for my ear drums.

"There was nothing wrong with what I had on before." I mentioned it to her.

"Breigh, stop complaining. There is nothing you can do about it now, we are here." she pulled into a parking spot.

"It's so crowded. Are you sure you want to go in there with all these people?" I tried to back out.

"Breigh! Get out of my car now!" she demanded me.

"Geez, what's your problem?" I asked.

"We are here to have fun and not complain. Got it." she said sternly.

"Yes mother." I replied sarcastically. Layla rolled her eyes at me.

"Leave your phone in the car." she told me.

"What if I need it later?" I pouted.

"Breigh, leave the damn thing in the car!" She was becoming frustrated with me. I did what I was told but I did not approve of it one bit.

As we walked towards the warehouse I had an eerie feeling. The cold wind blew across my face sending chills down my spine.

"All I see is a warehouse," I pointed out.

"Yeah, and?"

"I thought there was a haunted house or something."

"It's underground." Layla said.

"How did they build it underground?" I asked curiously.

"It was built over fifty years ago. Rumor has it that it used to be a dungeon type place where researchers would experiment with the mentally ill." she explained. "Once it was known what they were doing they shut them down."

"What kind of research?" I was intrigued by the story.

"They did research on their brains. They wanted to see why they were different from normal people. Except they didn't know what they were doing and a lot of people died because of these experiments." She went on.

"That is crazy. And they just left the place standing?"

"The warehouse is new. Back in the day when they tore the original building down, they didn't know there was a secret underground area. The people that put this together found it and made a whole theme out of it. I hear it really big down there."

"Wow," I looked at the warehouse and imagined how this place used to look. "How do you know all this?"

"Because I just made it all up," she smirked

I stopped walking and crossed my arms. "Really Layla?" I rolled my eyes at her.

Layla laughed at me. "You got to admit that was a good story."

"You really had me there." I admitted.

"I know nothing about this place. This is my first time here, just like you." she continued to laugh.

"You really suck sometimes."

"Yeah, but you love me."

"I can't believe I fell for that."

As soon as we made it into the warehouse, I thought I was going to have a panic attack. It was so crowded. The room was dark with green, purple, blue, orange laser lights flashing everywhere. Disco looking balls hanging from the ceilings. The music was so loud I could barely hear myself think. Loud screams were coming from the speakers like someone was getting murdered in real life and they blended it in with the music. A lot of people were dressed up in costumes or weird face paintings. The dance floor had people chest to chest it was so full. I couldn't see how some people didn't pass out from all the heat. This place just wasn't my cup of tea. I glanced at Layla who looked like she was at Disney World. Her eyes were big, and she looked so excited. I guess I can try to have a good time for her. If it wasn't for it being overly crowded it would be a cool place.

"Let's get us a drink first before heading to the dance floor." she yelled over the music.

"You want to go out there?" I asked her.

"You got to learn to let loose." she replied.

"I might die out there?" I told her.

She laughed at me, but I was being serious. She grabbed my hand and led me towards the bar. Trying not to shoulder bump anyone was nearly impossible. Surprisingly we found two empty stools next to each other so we both sat and waited on the bartender. I watched the dance floor in curiosity. I've never been to a place remotely like this, so it was all starting to become intriguing to me.

"What can I get you ladies to drink?" a familiar voice asked. I looked away from the dance floor with a big grin on my face.

"Arlo, hey." I managed to say.

"This is Arlo?" Layla asked with a big smile.

I just knew she was going to do something to embarrass me. "Yeah, he is the one who invited me to this really cool place." I said while I glanced around it one more time.

"He is a hottie, Breigh" she said without skipping a beat. I felt my face turn red from the embarrassment.

"Thank you." he chuckled while putting his head down. "I'm so glad you were able to make it Breigh. And you brought a friend with you." He looked at me with those deep blue eyes of his and I almost melted away.

"Best friend." Layla corrected him. She reached her hand out to shake his.

"Your first drink is on the house." he told us after he shook Layla's hand.

"I'll take a crown and coke." Layla told him without hesitation. He looked at me and smiled while waiting for me to decide what I wanted.

"I'll have the same." I told him. I didn't know what crown meant. I wasn't a drinker, but it sounded good.

"Two crown and cokes coming right up." He walked away and began making our drinks. I never drank hard liquor before so I was nervous about how it would make me feel.

"He is a major hottie, Breigh." Layla said again. Layla kept glancing at him while he made our drinks.

"He is." I admitted to her.

"I think you should go out with him." she blurted out.

I glanced at him to make sure he didn't hear her. He didn't. He was finishing up our drinks. You could barely hear the music anyways. "I don't know about all that." I replied to her. She was about to say something, but I signaled her to be quiet. Arlo was on his way back with our drinks.

"Here you ladies go." He sat our drinks in front of us.

Layla didn't hesitate to drink hers up. "I'll have another." she told him. He looked surprised. As did I. He looked at me waiting for me to tell him something.

"I'm good right now." I told him.

"One more crown and coke coming up." he said before walking away.

"Drink Breigh. We are supposed to be having fun." Layla told me. I took a sip of my drink, and it really wasn't that bad. The coke drowned out the liquor taste.

Before I knew it, I had already drunk three mixed drinks. I was starting to feel lightheaded. Everything was starting to spin.

"Let's go dance." Layla grabbed my hand and pulled me towards the dance floor without me agreeing to it.

We danced for what felt like hours. This was the most fun I have ever had in my life. Why haven't I ever done this before? I was never the fun type. Maybe I was trying so hard to make sure I was perfect so I could get my sister out of the hell hole we were living in. Layla was twirling me around and my stomach started to turn. I was about to blow chunks, and I couldn't stop myself. I turned to run but it didn't help and the person standing next to me got my dinner all over them.

"I am so sorry." I cried to them. The guy looked disgusted, and he was about to say something to me, but Layla saved the day by grabbing me and pulling me away.

"Are you okay?" Layla asked worried. "Let's get you to a restroom." she led the way. I hadn't noticed before, but she seemed to know where everything was. The bar, the restroom. It was my first time here and I didn't know where anything was. I just thought it was strange. They weren't in the open.

We were in the bathroom, and she wet a paper towel to help me clean my face.

"Have you been here before?" I asked curiously.

"No, never. Why?" she asked.

"You just seem to know your way around here so well. I would have been lost for days." I chuckled.

"They are all pretty much the same," she confessed. "Once you've been to one you've been to them all."

"I'm actually having a good time," I admitted. "Except for what I just did on the dance floor. That was embarrassing."

"It happens more often than you would believe." she chucked. "How are you feeling?"

"A lot better than before." I admitted.

"Feeling better enough to ask Arlo out?" she said with a grin on her face.

"Maybe not that much better." I confessed.

"Let's get back out there. But this time only water for you." she said.

"I agree." I told her.

Layla really surprised me tonight. She has been super friendly and has kept a good eye on me. We danced for a little while longer. Luckily, I didn't run into the guy I got sick of all over. I'm sure I ruined his night. Other than that, my night has been memorable so far.

Chapter Six

We returned to the bar for another drink.

"I'll have the usual and Breigh here will have a water." Layla told Arlo.

"Couldn't hang, could you?" he teased.

"Oh no, I'm not a drinker and I've already had too much." I confessed.

Arlo laughed at me. He had a distinctive laugh, and it made him so much cuter. "Have you two checked out the haunted house yet?" he asked, looking me directly in the eyes.

"I forgot all about that." Layla said. "We should go now Breigh."

"I don't know Layla," I told her. "You know I've never liked those things."

"You should go. It'll be fun." Arlo suggested.

"Yeah, let's go." Layla begged.

"Layla, you know I scare easy." I didn't want to admit that in front of Arlo, but I had to find a way out of it. I hate haunted houses. Things jumping out at you. What kind of fun was that?

"I'll tell you what, I'll go with you." Arlo offered. "That way if you get scared, I can protect you." He smiled at me, and I almost melted. Layla didn't say anything. She just looked at me big eyed with excitement like she was telling me to just go with her eyes.

"Okay." I finally caved. They both looked overly excited at each other. It almost made me feel a little suspicious.

"You two go ahead towards the elevator. I'm going to announce last call, and I'll let my friend know that I'll be right back." Arlo told us.

"Okay," we both said in sync.

Layla and I both headed towards the elevator. I would have never found it, but Layla walked us right to it. There was already a line waiting to go down. We stood there patiently waiting for our turn.

"Only six allowed at a time." said the muscled-up, bald headed bouncer that was controlling the haunted house extraction. His voice was just as scary as he looked. His black t shirt had no chance with his bulkiness. Maybe he could have used a couple sizes bigger. Unless that's the look he was going for. Scary and intimidating.

There were a group of friends who had to decide quickly which ones were going to get to go first.

"I wish they'd hurry up!" said an impatient Layla.

"I know right." I replied. After what felt like forever the first six loaded up and the remaining four continued to wait for the next turn.

"How long does it take to get through the whole haunted house?" asked a blonde headed girl who was dressed up like a sexy cat. She had on an all-black corset with what looked like black panties over her fishnet leggings. Her nose was painted black, and whiskers drawn on her face. Cat ears and cat tail were included in her attire. I get Halloween is a day to dress up but why would her man let her leave the house like that? I'm assuming the man who kept rubbing her ass was her man.

DEADLY NIGHT

"About thirty minutes." said the scary bouncer.

"So, we have to wait thirty minutes for them to get done?" complained the blond-haired person.

"Calm down babe." said the guy who has been all over her since we've been standing in line. He was in a black ninja costume so I couldn't see his entire face. He was brown-haired and blue-eyed. A black mask was tied around his face that covered his nose. He was tall and may have had one too many to drink.

"It's just going to take forever. I wanted to drink some more before last call." she told him.

"Last call for alcohol." We all heard Arlo's voice over the intercom.

"Oh great!" said the upset blond-haired girl as she crossed her arms.

"It's all good Sabrina. We have plenty at home for the after party." the other man that was with them announced. He was wearing a black tank top with some holey jeans. His arms and back were covered in tattoos. The guy's head was shaved but you could tell it was blonde. His light blue eyes kept looking back at Layla. He seemed to like what he saw despite him holding the other lady like they were a couple.

"If that's going to be enough." Sabrina rolled her eyes.

"Eugene is right." said the short chunky lady that was wrapped in Eugenes arms. "We have plenty." Her brown hair was pulled back into a ponytail. She didn't seem to dress up either. Her heavy black eyeliner and dark brown eye shadow really brought out her hazel eyes.

"Whatever Louise." Sabrina said rudely. It was very clear the two girls didn't like each other very much. Or at least Sabrina didn't like Louise.

The elevator doors finally opened, and everybody let out a sigh of relief. One by one they all loaded up in the elevator.

"Should we wait until the next one?" I asked Layla as I looked towards the bar for Arlo.

"For what?" she asked confused

"Arlo." I replied.

"This is the last ride down." the scary bouncer heard us talking. "You go now or not at all."

"Let's just go and you can call him afterwards." Layla suggested. I didn't like the idea of going at all. I only agreed to go because of Arlo and if he wasn't coming what was the point of me going? Layla kept staring at me with her sad eyes. Of course, it didn't take long for me to cave.

"Okay fine." I replied. I had a weird feeling while walking into the elevator. Something just didn't seem right. It was too late to go back now. The doors were closed, and we headed down.

Chapter Seven

On the way down in the elevator we learned that the ninja's name was Bryan, and he is in fact married to the cat Sabrina. Eugene and Louise have been dating for a year and she hopes to one day marry him. Eugene and Bryan have been best friends since grade school. It was actually a fifty-second argument between Sabrina and Louise that gave us all these details. I was right about them not liking each other.

I had to give Layla a stare that she knew all too well. That look that says, 'What did you get me into?' She shrugged her shoulders at me and gave me a sad pouty face expression. I rolled my eyes at her. I'm only glad these girls didn't start fist fighting. This elevator barely fit us in it and had no room for all that. If any of them touched me, they would end up in a hospital and not at an after party.

One by one we all exited the elevator. There was a sign on the door that was right in front of us that read **'ENTER IF YOU DARE'** in big red letters. It was made to believe it was written in blood. Bryan opened the door and was the first to enter. Sabrina held hands with Bryan as she followed close behind him.

"Should we go last?" Layla whispered to me.

"I don't care." I whispered back. "I just don't want to be too close to these people."

"I'll go behind you then," she told me. "I know how you hate scary things." Layla stood behind me as I followed Eugene and Louise. At least us being behind everyone we would know what to expect if something scary pops out and with Layla behind me I knew I was safe.

As soon as we walked into the first room chills went down my spine. There were dolls everywhere. Doll heads hanging from the ceiling. The lights were dim, but you could see the body parts of dolls glued to the walls. Faces, legs, and hands. It was creepy. Someone took a lot of time doing this and it was scary as hell to me. I wouldn't be able to look at dolls the same anymore. A creepy tune played on the loudspeaker giving the room an eerie feeling.

"This isn't even scary." I heard Eugene complain. He must be used to things like this.

"It's scary to me." Louise commented.

"That's because you're scared of everything." Sabrina said sarcastically.

I was really starting to not like this Sabrina chick. She seemed to always have something negative to say to Louise.

"Can we please get through this without you two arguing?" Bryan was getting frustrated with them. I didn't blame him. I was too. "The elevator was enough."

"These broads need to chill. They are ruining the experience." Layla whispered to me.

I didn't say anything back. I just nodded my head in agreement with her.

"I wonder how many dolls they had to buy to make this room?" Layla asked.

I glanced around the room trying to guess how many. "I'd say around two hundred. Then they had to pull them all apart and glue them to the wall."

"I'd guess four hundred."

The next room was completely different and a lot scarier than the doll room. The lights were bright. Blood covered the walls and floors of what was once a white room. There were tables that looked like chopped up body parts on them. A big muscled up man stood in the center of the room with a butcher's knife. He had on some black jeans and a long-sleeved white shirt that was covered in red paint of some sort. It was supposed to be blood as well. He had a black leather apron over his shirt and a mask that covered his whole face except his mouth. He was a lot scarier than the doll room. He acted like he didn't even know we were in his presence. He just continued cutting up body parts. The dummy on the table looked so real. If I didn't know any better, I would have believed that this room was completely real.

"Someone needs a tampon." Bryan joked.

"Shut up." a scared Sabrina nudged him in the chest with her elbow.

Eugene was laughing like he was at a comedy club or something. Layla and I both rolled our eyes. It was nowhere near funny. These guys were so immature. Eugene almost tripped over a severed hand on the ground. He picked it up and threw it at the butcher.

"What the hell did you do that for?" Layla yelled at him.

"Mind your business." He told her as he and Bryan both laughed at what he had done. I had a feeling Eugene would later regret what he had done.

It was hard trying not to look at the butcher. He stared at us as we all walked by him slowly, scared that he might take a swing on us or something. Layla grabbed my hand and squeezed it tightly. I could tell that this room scared her as well. Layla and I were the last to exit the room and right before we did the butcher threw his knife in our direction stabbing it into the wall. We both screamed and ran bumping into Eugene and Louise.

"Watch were you're going." Louise said with an attitude.

"It was an accident." Layla snapped rudely back at her.

They could barely see each other because the next room we entered was pitch black and every couple of seconds a flash of light would brighten up the room for a second.

"I can't see anything." Sabrina complained. "I better not have a seizure."

"This is so cool." Eugene said with excitement. "I think we should do our room like this Louise."

"I don't like this." I told Layla as I held her hand tighter. I had a weird feeling something wasn't right.

"It will all be over soon." she assured me.

We heard Sabrina scream, and I jumped. Eugene and Bryan began laughing. Sabrina slapped Bryan in the chest, "That wasn't funny," she pouted. She ran into a mannequin dressed all in black.

"Then why am I laughing so hard? Eugene gave her a tough time.

"Get your friend before I hit him, Bryan!"

"Before you hit who?" Louise jumped in to defend her man.

"No one was talking to you," Sabrina snapped back.

"Here we go again," Layla said under her breath.

"You two need to stop. We are trying to have a fun time, and this battle between the two of you is so childish!" Bryan scorned them both.

Neither one of them said anything back.

You could barely see in this room, but I felt like someone was watching me. I started to get an unsettling feeling.

"I feel like I'm getting dizzy." Louise started to panic.

"Don't be such a baby." Eugene told her.

"I'm scared." she told him.

"I know. You're squeezing my hand too tight." He sounded like he was in pain.

"What are you talking about?" she asked him. "I'm not holding your hand."

"Then who has my hand?" he asked with a trembling voice.

Just then all the lights came on and we all could see the butcher holding Eugene's hand. He chuckled and took his butcher knife and cut right through his wrist like it was butter. Everybody screamed and started to scatter looking for a way out. Eugene fell to the ground screaming in agonizing pain. He held his arm up watching the blood squirt out. The butcher looked at me and Layla and smirked. We were both crying and screaming not knowing what was going to happen to us. Layla blocked me like she was protecting me. The butcher turned around and slowly walked back to the room we had just come from.

Chapter Eight

Everybody ran to Eugene except for Sabrina who was standing in the corner in shock.

"Are you okay?" Bryan asked frantically.

Eugene couldn't reply because he was still screaming in pain. Bryan took his cloth mask off and wrapped it around Eugenes arm giving him a tourniquet.

"This should help stop the bleeding" Bryan told him.

Eugene looked as if it hurt more putting the tourniquet on than actually losing a hand.

"Why the hell would he do that?" asked a scared Layla. I was right by her side crying and shaking. I had never seen anything like this before. Except maybe in the movies and even then, I could barely stomach it.

"Because he was taunting him." Sabrina blurted out. "You should have listened when we said to stop."

"Sabrina! Shut up right now." Bryan shouted at her. Sabrina rolled her eyes at Bryan but didn't say another word.

"Did anyone bring their phone?" asked Louise who was struggling to talk through the tears as she was knelt beside Eugene. She was holding his head in his lap rubbing his hair trying to calm him down. She was still horrified herself.

DEADLY NIGHT 41

"We left ours in the car." I said to her. I wish I never listened to Layla about leaving my phone in the car. I never go anywhere without it.

"We didn't bring ours in either." Bryan responded to her.

"We need to get him to the hospital fast." Louise's voice was trembling. "How are we supposed to do that if nobody has a damn phone on them?" Louise started to panic.

"Louise, I need you to calm down. You're not helping anyone when you start freaking out. We are going to have to find a way out of here." Bryan glanced around the room. "I think we need to keep going forward."

"I'm not going back that way." Sabrina started to shout. You could tell by her trembling voice she was scared. Just like the rest of us.

"So, are we supposed to keep going forward? We don't know what lies ahead for us." I asked looking at the scary entrance.

"That guy went back that way." Sabrina said sobbing. "He might still be there just waiting to finish us all off."

"She's right. I'm not going back that way either." I added my opinion.

"We don't know how long it's going to take to find the exit Breigh." Layla was disappointed with my opinion. "This man needs to get to the hospital now."

At the moment I could care less about anyone else. I didn't know these people. Eugene brought this on himself and as far as we knew the butcher did what he came for. He could have hurt all of us, but he only attacked Eugene.

"Then you can go that way, and I'll go the other way." I told her. Sabrina was right about the butcher going back to the room we just left. We didn't know if he was still there or not. I wasn't willing to take that chance.

"I'm not leaving you." she said sincerely. "I'm going wherever you are going."

"Are you two lesbians?" blurted out Bryan. Louise slapped his shoulder.

"Really Bryan?" she said to him. "Is that what's important to you right now?"

"No, we are just best friends. Not that it is any of your business." Layla told him rudely.

"This is not the time to be discussing sexual orientation. We need to get Eugene to a hospital now. So can someone please figure out a way out of here." Louise was getting impatient.

"I'm not going back the way we came." Eugene struggled to say. "I'm not giving that psycho a chance to finish the job."

"We'll need to do something before he comes back. It's like we're just standing around waiting for him to come back." Sabrina pointed out.

"Eugene, can you stand up?" Bryan asked.

"I don't know man. I've lost a lot of blood." he told him. "I'm feeling really weak."

"Here I'll help you up." Bryan offered. Bryan and Louise helped Eugene up. Eugene put his arm around Bryan's neck to steady himself and his injured arm around Louise.

"Where's his hand?" Layla asked. "They might be able to sew it back on at the hospital."

"You're right." I told her. I remembered watching that on a medical show before. They have a certain amount of time to do it I believe.

Everyone started looking around the room. There wasn't much in here. With the lights on it wasn't spooky at all. Just some tables along the wall and some spooky posters. There were two mannequins inside the room. The light effect made it seem so much scarier.

"It's not here." Sabrina cried out as she looked under one table.

"Maybe he took it." I suggested. Just the thought of him keeping it made me sick. What would he need it for? A souvenir? That was gross.

"What kind of psycho steals someone's severed hand?" Eugene asked as he started to look pale. He was either hiding the pain well. Or maybe he was starting to go numb.

"The kind that chops one off." Layla answered him.

Everyone looked at her surprised by her response. I'll admit her sense of humor usually came at the wrong time. Just like right now. "What?" She looked at me and shrugged her shoulders. I just shook my head at her.

"Let's just get you out of here and hopefully the police find it when they come to arrest that psychopath." Bryan suggested.

The rest of us followed Bryan as he and Louise led Eugene to the other room. Out of nowhere the lights went out and sent us all into a panic. We were all screaming at the top of our lungs as we all scattered to hide.

I could hear Bryan saying something, but I couldn't make it out over everyone's screams.

The lights came back on, and I yelled for Layla. "Layla, where are you?" I was so scared something had happened to her.

"Right here." she answered, still crying. She was at the other end of the room under a table. I ran to her side making sure she was okay. Bryan was helping Eugene off the floor. Sabrina ran to him and helped him with Eugene.

"Someone knocked me down." Eugene struggled to say. He was starting to look pale.

"I felt someone too. I think it was that butcher again." Bryan said. "He grabbed me and threw me to the ground."

"The other girl. Where is she at?" I asked them while I was looking around the room for her. Everyone else joined me.

"LOUISE!" Eugene yelled for her. "LOUISE WHERE ARE YOU?"

"Where could she have gone?" Sabrina asked. "Do you think he took her?

"I have no idea." Bryan answered her. "I pray that he didn't."

Just then the door we were going to walk through opened and the butcher walked out slowly with something in his hand. We all struggled to get to the other end of the room while he threw something in the middle of the floor and slowly walked away back to where he came from.

"What the hell is that?" I screamed.

"I don't know." Layla responded just as scared as I was.

"Bryan, go look at it." Sabrina told him as her body was shaking. "I'm too scared to move."

He didn't respond but did what he was asked. He slowly walked towards the object on the ground keeping an eye on the door just in case the butcher came back. When Bryan reached the object, he had to look away quickly to vomit.

"What is it?" Sabrina asked scared. She started to slowly walk towards him.

"Don't come over here!" he demanded of her. "Everyone just stay where you are!"

"Why, what is it?" Layla asked curiously. Bryan was knelt over and put his hand up to signal us not to come towards him.

"Bryan! What the hell is it?" Eugene demanded to know. He used what strength he had left and stumbled towards Bryan.

Bryan tried to stop him by jumping in front of him. "I wouldn't look at it if I were you, Eugene."

"Get the hell out of my way!" Eugene demanded Bryan, then with his good arm pushed him out of the way. Just by looking at these two guys Bryan didn't put too much effort into keeping Eugene back. He was twice his size and with the amount of blood Eugene had lost even though I knew he was too weak to have pushed anyone out of the way.

Eugene fell to his knees when he realized what it was Bryan didn't want anyone to see.

It was Louise's head.

Chapter Nine

Layla tried to calm down Eugene who was crying uncontrollably on the ground next to Louise's head. I could tell by the way he howled that he loved her deeply. It was unbearable to watch. Layla was knelt beside him with her hand on his back, but she wouldn't look in the direction of Louise's head. Bryan was consoling Sabrina who was hyperventilating in a corner. I was still in shock. I didn't want to move, and my body was shaking. I didn't understand why this was happening to us. We had to figure out a way to get out of here fast before we were all dead. I walked towards the door we first entered through. I turned the knob, and it was locked. We were trapped here.

"Shit." I said out loud. I was hoping nobody heard me. I didn't want everyone to start freaking out again.

"What's wrong?" Layla looked up at me. She always did have good hearing.

"The door is locked." I cried to her.

"You've got to be kidding me." Layla jumped up and ran to the door. She turned the knob as if she didn't believe me and had to see for herself. She started to cry as she banged on the door. "Let us out of here!" she shouted. Nobody responded of course. We were exactly where they wanted us.

"How are we supposed to get out of here?" Sabrina started to hyperventilate again after Bryan just got her to calm down.

DEADLY NIGHT

"We'll figure a way out." Bryan assured her. "We'll be out of here soon I promise."

Sabrina started crying uncontrollably and Bryan smothered her head into his chest as he rubbed on her back. "It's going to be okay baby. We are going to be okay."

He must have loved her deeply. He was gentle with her. Was it just a reaction of him being scared as well or was he like this all the time? I've read somewhere that men seem to be more affectionate when they are scared. He didn't seem like an asshole.

Eugene on the other hand, seemed like the dog type of guy. Now that his girlfriend was dead, he seemed to act like he loved her and nobody else came above her. He was a jerk to her in the elevator. Maybe it's true what they say, you don't know what you have until it is gone. Even though it was his fault Louise was killed.

"We have no choice but to keep going." Layla said.

"Why can't we just stay here?" I didn't like the idea of venturing off. I'm sure someone would have noticed they were missing by now and would have called the police.

"Why? So that guy can come back and kill us off one by one?" Layla complained.

I looked at Eugene who was still on the ground crying. I then looked at Bryan and Sabrina. Bryan was still holding her tightly. I hated to admit it, but Layla was right. We have already been attacked twice and no telling if the guy was going to return to finish us all off.

"Your friend is right. We must keep moving before he returns." Bryan added his opinion.

"But we don't know what is going to happen if we go through that door." Sabrina was scared. We all knew this would be a big risk. We stay here and we'll be like sitting ducks. No telling who was going to be next. If we continue, we may find the way out of here.

"I'm not leaving Louise behind." Eugene blurted out still crying. I didn't blame him for feeling that way. I was hysterical when Mylah first went missing. I've learned to deal with my pain. I feel it every day, but I've gotten better. Then again, Mylah is only missing. My gut told me she was gone but there is no evidence of that. Her body was never recovered so the police just have her listed as a missing person.

"It's just her head." Sabrina mumbled. I heard her and gave her a dirty look. She seen me and shrugged her shoulders.

"Eugene, we have to save ourselves right now." Bryan told him while touching his shoulder. "Louise is gone. We have to leave before that guy comes back and kills one of us."

"Get off of me!" Eugene pushed Bryan away from him. "I can't just leave her here like this."

"Just leave him." Sabrina blurted out. I swear this girl was really starting to get my blood boiling. She seemed selfish.

"We are not leaving him." Bryan turned to her and yelled. She could tell by the look in his eyes that wasn't the right thing to say to him. She didn't respond to him.

"Whatever we are going to do we need to do it fast." I pointed out. Everybody looked at Eugene. We knew he didn't want to leave but he wasn't thinking rational right now. Bryan didn't want to leave him behind but right now it was more about our survival. The ones that were still alive.

"Eugene, you know I can't do this without you." he began to say. "You have been by my side through all of life's triumphs. I need you now more than ever, brother. I know you are hurting but we need to get you out of here so you can go home to your daughter. It's what Louise would have wanted, and you know that."

It was heartbreaking knowing that a child lost their mother tonight in a gruesome death. Eugene cried a little harder knowing that Bryan was right. He kissed the head of his dead girlfriend and slowly stood up with Bryans help. Nobody said anything. We all just started walking towards the only way we could go.

Chapter Ten

With all the lights on nothing seemed as scary. We made it through two rooms with nothing happening to any of us. Fake body parts hung from the ceiling of one of the rooms and the other room just looked like a bad science experiment gone wrong. I think deep down we all felt a little safer. Maybe the butcher was done. Maybe Sabrina was right, and Eugene offended him, so he did what he did. He had some anger issues for sure. One disturbed person to cut someone's head off. Maybe he can work on that in prison when he gets there.

As we were entering the next room, I noticed a bunch of balloons blocking the way. We had to push them out of the way just to get through. Bryan pulled a pocketknife out of his pocket and started popping some of them to make it easier to get through. When we finally made it through, the room was dark with a bunch of colorful neon writings on the wall. **'Welcome to the fun house'** was written in big green and blue letters. This could only mean one thing and I was instantly scared.

Clowns!

I hated clowns. Layla knew how terrified I was of them. She has seen me scream like a little girl on multiple occasions involving clowns.

"Are you okay?" she asked concerned when she realized what I already knew.

I couldn't say anything. I just nodded my head yes. She knew I was lying. She grabbed my hand tightly and walked beside me. Clowns gave me the creeps. They dress up as happy people but are really evil people. I remember when Mylah and I arrived at our first foster care family, and they had a little party to welcome us. They hired a clown. Mylah and I both had nightmares for a month. Mylah would wake up screaming every night claiming the clowns were going to get her. Eventually, the family couldn't handle it anymore and they sent us to a different family. I watched one too many killer clown movies to ever trust a clown. They just really terrified the fuck out of me.

As we got further into the room there were writings all over the wall. One gave me chills down my spine.

Death has a face

I started to feel cold and wanted to leave this room in a hurry. A bad feeling in my gut told me I wasn't safe in this room. Barrels were piled on top of each other with neon green paint covered on them. **Toxic** was written across them in black letters.

"This actually looks really cool." Sabrina said, breaking the silence. I didn't think this room was cool at all. I cringed at the thought of clowns.

"Not cool enough to stick around in." Bryan told her. "Let's keep going. This room is giving me the creeps."

I agreed with Bryan. This room was creepy and dark. The neon lights just made it even scarier.

"What is that in the corner?" Eugene struggled to lift his arm up to point to the right of us.

All we could really see was a face painted in neon colors. It blended in with the room well. I wouldn't have noticed it if Eugene hadn't pointed it out.

"That looks creepy." Layla said under her breath. She wasn't exaggerating. It was creepy alright.

"It's just the wall painted." Sabrina confirmed as she slowly walked towards the face. "Wait." she uttered. She reached her hand out to touch it.

"Sabrina don't!" Bryan yelled at her, but it was too late.

The face moved and we all saw that it was a clown. It had a knife in its hand and with a quickness it cut Sabrina's throat. I started to scream hysterically.

"SABRINA!" Bryan cried out. He dropped Eugene and ran to her. The clown was laughing a wicked laugh and started dancing. It was proud of itself. Bryan swung at the clown, but it was obvious it was faster than Bryan. It dodged his hit three times and giggled at Bryan after each attempt. Bryan finally got one hit in, and the clown fell to the floor.

The clown looked angry as he slowly got back on his feet. He lunged at Bryan with the knife but missed him. Bryan swung again. Damn he missed the clown again. This time the clown didn't miss Bryan by cutting him across his chest. Bryan cried out in pain as he fell to the floor grabbing his chest. Layla out of nowhere jumped on the clowns back.

What the hell was she doing? "Layla, stop." I cried out to her.

It was too late. She was trying to choke the clown from behind while he was running into walls trying to get her off it's back. Finally, the clown succeeded when he threw Layla in the pile of barrels, and she fell to the ground. The clown was about to stab her when I ran towards him and pushed him away from her. The clown ran towards me and tackled me to the ground. He knocked the breath out of me. The clown sat on top of me so I couldn't move. He started giggling as he pulled his knife

DEADLY NIGHT   53

out once more. I thought this is where my story ended. All I could think about was Mylah. The clown was about to stab me when someone stopped him. The clown went flying on the floor and started wrestling with someone else. I couldn't tell at first. I crawled to Layla who was still on the ground. I looked to see who saved me. To my surprise it was Eugene. The clown had Eugene pinned to the ground and stabbed him two times before Bryan kicked the clown in the face. The clown seemed to be knocked out. Bryan grabbed Eugene and dragged him away from the clown. Luckily, he was still alive.

"You are going to be okay." Bryan told him as he held him tightly. "Just hang on buddy."

"I'm feeling really weak." Eugene struggled to say.

I crawled towards them leaving Layla alone. I had to help Eugene. My adrenaline was in full force now and I couldn't just sit there and cry while people were dying.

"Where are you stabbed at." I asked Eugene.

He didn't respond.

"His arm and in the stomach." Bryan answered him.

I took my top off revealing my white spaghetti strapped underneath it. I wrapped it around Eugene's arm to help stop the bleeding. I knew it would help him for a short time. If we couldn't get him to a hospital soon, he would certainly bleed out. He had too many injuries.

"I don't have anything for his stomach." I told Bryan.

"It's okay. Thank you." Bryan told me. I could tell he was crying although he tried to hide it. I didn't judge him for it. It made me feel worse.

"It's the least I can do." I told him wishing I could have done more. "He saved my life."

"BREIGH!" Layla's scream startled us both. We both looked and the clown had a chain wrapped around Layla's throat and started laughing.

"LAYLA!" I screamed her name and jumped up. Layla had her arm reached out for me to grab it as the clown dragged her out of the room we were in. He continued to laugh as I started to run after them. I almost had Layla's hand until something grabbed me pulling me back.

"NO!" I cried out.

It was Bryan. He had me by the waist and wouldn't let me go. I squirmed to get away from him, but he was a lot stronger than I thought.

"What are you doing? Let me go!" I demanded him. I could still hear Layla's screams. I still had a chance to save her. Why is he stopping me from saving her?

"Don't try playing the hero, it's only going to get you killed." he told me.

"I could have saved her." I cried to him.

"You could have saved her as much as I could have saved my wife." He pointed at his wife's dead body before walking towards her and sitting on the ground to hold her one last time.

"She's all I have." I cried.

"And my wife and Eugene are all I have in this world." he confessed. He kissed his wife's forehead. "If you want to go get yourself killed then go. I won't stop you. If she is really your best friend, she would want you to get out of this alive." He had a point.

I couldn't hear Layla screaming anymore so I didn't know whether she was alive or dead. I had to pull myself together and

DEADLY NIGHT

get out of here alive. Tears rolled down my eyes. I was scared as hell. I swear I hate Halloween.

"If you're not going, will you help me, get Eugene up?" Bryan asked me.

I didn't say anything back. Just followed him to Eugene. I kicked something on the ground as I was walking. I bent down to pick it up.

"It's the clowns knife." I showed Bryan.

"Keep it. You may need it." he told me.

I stuck the blade in my back pocket and helped him bring Eugene to his feet. "Do you think we are going to make it out of here alive?" I asked Bryan as we made our way to the next room.

"I really hope so. At least for Eugene's sake." he replied. "Killing that clown and butcher will be the last thing I do." he told me.

"How old is his daughter?" I asked to change the subject. He looked at me confused. "I overheard what you said to him earlier."

"She's five." Eugene whispered. He sounded like he may have lost a lot of blood. "She has her mama's beautiful eyes and her daddy's attitude." he chuckled.

"She definitely has your attitude." Bryan teased him.

Eugene started to laugh but it became too painful, and he started coughing up blood instead.

"We have to get him somewhere to rest quick." Bryan told me.

We headed in the direction of the next room again, not knowing what lies ahead for us. Everything has been crazy so far. Knowing that there were two people after us instead of one made our chances of survival a lot slimmer. The thought did cross my mind that I might not be getting out of here alive.

Chapter Eleven

We sat on the floor in a room that had a chain link fence going along the wall in it. I wondered what it was supposed to be. It was a bigger room. Maybe it was a storage room? It was a little odd for them to have a storage room as part of their haunted house attraction. Maybe they forgot a room? Or they had already started tearing it down before we came down. Then again what would I know? This is my first and even if I survive, this will be my last experience with a haunted house.

There was a box of tools in one of the corners of the room. It didn't take long for Bryan to go through it. He found a couple of wrenches and some screw drivers.

"You can use this one as a weapon." he told me as he handed me a screwdriver with a yellow and black handle.

I stuck it in my back pocket along with the knife. We all sat along the fence towards the middle of the room. The room was dim with the lights flickering. I suggested we keep moving but Bryan didn't think it was a good idea because Eugene couldn't take the pain anymore. I think Bryan knew deep down that Eugene wasn't going to make it. I sat there quietly crying. Wishing that Layla was here with me. Or even Mylah. Wishing I never came to this stupid party. I could be at home reading a book or watching a movie but instead I'm sitting here with two men I didn't even know. After losing three others we entered in here with and another one is slowly dying. I looked over at them. I hadn't noticed before, but Bryan was ripped. He looked as if he worked out every day. He took the top layer of his costume off and wrapped it around Eugene's waist. I could see the cut Bryan had against his chest. It looked deep but it didn't seem to bother him. Or he just didn't want us to know he was hurt too. The blood was dripping down to his stomach.

"Do you need anything?" I asked him as I pointed at his chest. He looked at me and shook his head no. Then continued to give Eugene all his attention.

"Do you remember my wedding day?" Bryan asked Eugene.

"How could I ever forget." Eugene tried to giggle but started coughing instead.

"One of the best days of my life." Bryan said smiling.

"Sabrina looked beautiful." Eugene said to him.

"She sure did." Bryan replied.

"She was too good for you." Eugene told him as he tried to smile.

"She was perfect for me." Bryan corrected him.

"I hooked up with the maid of honor that night." Eugene confessed.

"With Samantha?" Bryan sounded shocked. "You're lying."

"No," Eugene shook his head. "I really did." They both started laughing.

"She was always an uptight bitch." Bryan told him.

"Well, her attitude changed after a night with me." Eugene joked.

"Sabrina would have had a field day with you if she knew that." Bryan admitted. I could see a tear roll down his cheek.

DEADLY NIGHT

"That's why I never told her." Eugene confessed. "She really was a good person."

"She was the best." Bryan agreed with Eugene.

"She straightened your ass up." Eugene told him.

"Like Louise did to you." Bryan replied.

"I should have married her." Eugene sounded regretful.

"You should have. She was perfect for you." Bryan told him. "And she gave you a beautiful daughter."

"From a one-night stand at that." They both laughed.

"How did you get so lucky. You have a one-night stand with someone, and they disappear for three years and suddenly, they are back in your life with the child you made together. That's just crazy man." Bryan wondered.

"Just my luck I guess." Eugene smiled. "Do me a favor Bryan."

"Anything brother." Bryan answered.

"Take care of Bella for me." Eugene sounded sincere. He knew he wasn't making it out of here.

"I'm not going to have to. We are getting out of here alive." Bryan told him. He started to cry even more now.

I imagined what it would have been like if Mylah was here with me. I would be telling her the same thing. Tears escaped my eyes. I brushed them away quickly before any of them noticed I was crying along with them.

"Bryan shut up and tell me you will take care of Bella for me." Eugene told him as he started to cough again.

"I promise Eugene. I'm going to take care of her like she is my own. She is never going to forget you or Louise for as long as I live." Bryan promised him.

"Thanks, Bryan, for everything you've ever down for me." Eugene closed his eyes.

"Eugene!" Bryan started to panic as he shook him.

"Calm down I'm still alive." Eugene started laughing. Bryan let out a sigh of relief. "What's your story pirate?" He looked over at me. I quickly wiped my eyes hoping they didn't see me crying.

"Who me?" I answered.

"Yeah, you were a pirate, right?" Eugene asked.

"Actually, I was..." I started to say. Then I figured, why even try to correct him. It wasn't even important anymore. "Yeah, I was a pirate."

"So, what's your story?" Eugene asked again.

"I came here with my sister's best friend hoping for a good night. This is my very first haunted attraction." I confessed to them.

"Why not your sister?" Eugene asked.

"Excuse me?"

"You came with your sister's best friend. Why didn't your sister come?"

I put my head down not wanting to say it out loud, but I felt a connection with these guys. They have both saved me. "She has been missing for one year today."

"Really?" Bryan asked, shocked.

"The police have no leads or a clue as to where she could be?" Bryan asked.

"They just think she doesn't want to be found but I think someone did something to her." I told him softly. I was hard to talk about. I lost hope that she was still alive the day she went missing. I knew my sister like I knew the back of my hand and she would never just disappear without reaching out to me. Or even Layla for that matter.

"Like who?" Eugene asked curiously.

"Our mother." I blurted out. "That's the only person I knew would want to hurt her."

Eugene raised an eyebrow. "Why would you think your mother would harm your sister?"

"Well, where to begin." I began to say. "My sister Mylah and I grew up in the system starting from a very young age. When I turned eighteen, I got custody of her."

"That's awesome." said Bryan. "There's not too many people that would raise a sibling."

"She disappeared last Halloween after reconnecting with our mother. I tried to warn her not to feed into her lies, but she didn't listen." I confessed.

"I'm sorry to hear that." Eugene said. "I guess we all lost someone tonight." he said while holding his chest.

"I didn't want to come here tonight. I wanted to stay home and read a book." I confessed. "But Layla wanted me to come out to enjoy myself." I shocked myself when I started laughing. "And what a blast it has been."

Bryan and Eugene both started laughing as well. I think we were just tired of crying that it all turned into laughs. The emotional rollercoaster we've been on tonight was unimaginable. And here we were, sitting here resting knowing there were people trying to kill us. Maybe we were the crazy ones?

We all stopped laughing instantly when a noise interrupted us.

"Shhh, what is that?" asked Bryan.

We all listened to try to figure it out.

"I don't know." I replied. "It sounds like..." I looked at Bryan and he looked back on me. We figured it out at the same time and said it out loud together.

"CHAINSAW!"

Chapter Twelve

Bryan and I jumped to our feet not knowing what to expect. All we knew for sure was someone was coming for us with a chainsaw.

"Whatever happens we have to fight back." Bryan told me.

I nodded my head yes even though I was scared. My heart started racing and my body was shaky. I was in no shape to fight back. There were only three of us left. Was this the end for me? I barely survived this far.

The clown came busting through the door with a chainsaw like we thought we heard. It was so much louder up close and personal. He went straight for Bryan. Bryan dodged the chainsaw multiple times. The clown kept giggling like it was all a game.

I grabbed the knife out of my back pocket and snuck up behind the clown. I stabbed the clown in the back. He dropped the chainsaw on his way to the ground letting out a cry.

Bryan seen this as the opportunity to attack him while he was down. Byran grabbed the clown and started punching him repeatedly in the face. Bryan let him go thinking he had enough.

The clown jumped up to defend himself. He tackled Bryan and they both fell to the ground. I watched in panic as they wrestled with each other. Bryan was the strongest out of us three.

If he dies, Eugene and I won't stand a chance. I had to think of something to help him.

"Breigh, get the knife!" Bryan yelled at me.

The clown was now on top of Bryan and laughing his creepy laugh after each hit, he gave him. I ran towards the knife that fell out of the clown's back, but something stopped me in my tracks.

The butcher.

He walked up to me and grabbed me by the throat without any hesitation. Before I knew it, he had me pinned against the wall. I kept swinging at him and kicking him, but it didn't faze him. I could feel my body growing weaker as he was draining the life out of me. I had to think of something quick before he killed me.

"SCREWDRIVER!" Bryan yelled. He was still wrestling with the clown, but it looked like he was winning.

I forgot I had that. With what strength I had left I reached for the screwdriver in my back pocket and stabbed it as hard as I could into the side of the butcher's head.

He released me in an instant. I fell to the ground hard gasping for air. This must be what a fish out of water feels like. I tried to crawl away, but I could barely move.

The butcher pulled the screwdriver out of his head and dropped it on the ground without even blinking. I moved away from him slowly. He looked at me like he was pissed. Why won't this man go down. I thought he would have died instantly.

"Screwdriver only pissed him off more." I managed to yell at Brian while keeping an eye on the butcher.

"Kinda busy." he yelled back at me.

I made it to my feet and walked backwards as the butcher slowly came towards me. I noticed the screwdriver laying on the

DEADLY NIGHT

ground behind him. I had to figure out a way to get to it before he got to me. I glanced quickly around the room trying to think. The chainsaw was still running on the ground close to me. I had to make a move quick if I wanted to live. I turned around and ran to the chainsaw and grabbed the handle to lift it up. It was heavier than I thought it would be, but I got it lifted. I swung it at the butcher, but he just smiled at me as he dodged all my attempts.

I gave up finally and just threw the damn thing at him. Which turned out to be a good thing. The chainsaw took a big chunk out of his left arm. His injury slowed him down enough for me to grab the screwdriver. I ran behind him and just started stabbing him repeatedly with it. I stabbed him until he fell forward on the ground. He rolled over onto his back and I started stabbing him in his chest. I wanted to make sure he was dead.

When he stopped moving, I gave him a couple more stabs just in case. My white spaghetti strapped shirt was saturated in blood. I could feel his blood dripping from my face. I sat on top of him until I could catch my breath. I looked at Bryan who was still wrestling with the clown but only this time it looked like the clown was getting the best of him. I pulled the screwdriver out of the butcher's chest and held it tightly. I was hoping I could do the same thing to the clown like I did the butcher.

The clown was standing over Bryan now so I stood up to sneak behind him but before I could Eugene tackled the clown to the ground and they both fell on the chainsaw. Blood squirted everywhere as we heard both of their screams.

"Eugene!" Bryan cried out but it was too late.

The screams had stopped. The chainsaw went through Eugene's stomach, and he was dead within seconds. I could hear the pain Bryan was feeling through his cries. It was how I cried when I last saw Mylah. Eugene was his best friend, like Mylah was mine. I turned the chainsaw off, and I went to Bryan who was sobbing on the ground next to Eugene's body and wrapped my arms around him.

"It's going to be okay." I told him. "We are going to get out of here and you are going to keep your promise to him."

Bryan didn't respond to me. I didn't need him to though. I wanted him to let all his hurt out. Watching his wife and best friend get murdered in the same night could bring the strongest person in the world to their knees and destroy them. Bryan was my hero, and I couldn't let him give up now. I could feel that we were close to getting out of here.

Chapter Thirteen

"I think the exit is close by." Bryan muttered.

"Do you need more time here?" I asked him.

We both looked at Eugene's body. I knew this was hard for him even though he tried to put on a strong face. Witnessing your best friend being killed is traumatizing.

"I need to get to Bella." he said. "I have a promise to keep."

We both climbed off the floor after trying to catch our breath for the past fifteen minutes. I felt weak and exhausted. Bryan had a lot of injuries, and I didn't know the severity of them. He put on a strong demeanor, but I could tell he was in pain.

We saw a door that said exit. Could this be it? Are we finally getting out of here? If I was able to run, I would have. I wanted out of this nightmare as fast as I could. As we opened the door with high hopes, we were disappointed. Instead, there stood Arlo. He looked different than how he did when I had seen him last. He was wearing a white tank top showing his muscles off. He was now wearing jeans with holes in them and his hair was down. It was longer than I imagined it to be. He must have been waiting for me.

"Arlo!" I shouted with excitement. I used what energy I had left and ran to him. I wrapped my arms around him to hug him. I haven't been this happy to see anyone in my life.

"Oh man, we are glad to see you. You don't know the hell we've been through tonight." Bryan kept talking but his words started to fade when I looked up into Arlo's eyes. He wasn't the same. His eyes were dark and cold. Something wasn't right. He just kept staring at me not saying anything or moving. He was emotionless. He looked evil. Like he wanted to hurt me.

"Arlo." I mumbled his name hoping I was wrong.

"My name is Daegan." he replied.

My eyes grew wide. I tried to back away from him, but it was too late. He grabbed my arm and then punched me hard in the face and knocked me out.

I finally woke up to find Daegan and Bryan both laid out on the ground. An ache from my face still lingered from where Daegan hit me. I crawled to Bryan and checked his pulse. Barely faint. I had to get him to help fast. He wasn't going to make it much longer. I saw another exit door that was just across from the room. Was it another false exit? Was someone else going to be standing on the other side of it? I hesitated at first, but I knew I had to take the risk for Bryan, or he was going to die. I got up and ran to the door. Safety was so close. I was almost there but something stopped me. There was a picture on the door. A picture of me and Mylah. I stopped running as I looked at the picture confused. Why was there a picture of me and Mylah taped to the door? I was confused more than ever as I walked up to the picture to get a better look. Mylah and I were kids dressed up in cheap costumes. Our mom put capes on us and told us we were super heroes. How did this picture get here? I was startled by someone clapping behind me, so I quickly turned to look.

"Layla?" I said in disbelief. "You're alive?" I was about to run to her, but something told me not to.

"No thanks to you." she said sarcastically.

"I wanted to go back for you, but Bryan wouldn't let me." I tried to explain.

"Yeah sure, whatever!" She didn't believe me.

"I swear Layla." I pleaded with her. "You don't look hurt. How did you escape?" I was starting to feel suspicious. How come she wasn't injured? Not even a scratch on her anywhere. She didn't look afraid. As a matter of fact, she looked like she was up to no good. "What is going on Layla?" I asked her softly.

"I've been keeping this secret from you for a whole year now Breigh and I really need to get it off my chest."

"What secret?" I asked her nervously.

She started to slowly walk towards me, and I slowly backed away. "A secret about Mylah." She looked up at me and smiled.

"Layla, you don't want to do this." I tried to stop her, but she refused to shut up.

"I was there the night Mylah disappeared. Or should I say when she was killed."

"Layla, stop talking please. I beg you to stop." I begged her again.

"No Breigh!" she shouted at me. "Tell me what happened to Mylah! I sat around for a whole year while everyone drove themselves crazy looking for her. I wanted to go to the police every single day to turn you in because I know you know what happened to her, but Daegan begged me not to. He had other plans for you." she confessed.

"You're right Layla." I smirked at her. "I killed Mylah."

Chapter Fourteen

One Year Ago

I paced back and forth in the living room after Mylah stormed out of the apartment. I was furious with her. How could she do this to me? After all I had done for her. I gave up my life to give her one and she turns her back on me for the person who abandoned us. My hands were trembling with anger. I let out a high-pitched scream to help release some of the anger. A picture hung on the wall in the living room of me and my sister during happier times. I couldn't stand the sight of her. I punched the picture, and my knuckles started bleeding from the busted glass. I couldn't feel it. The anger wouldn't let me. I stared at the blood for a few seconds. It shouldn't be me bleeding. It should be Mylah. She deserved to be hurt. I'm not the one who betrayed her.

I wanted to know why? Why did she choose our so-called mother over me? I grabbed my coat and keys and decided to follow her. I wanted answers and I wanted answers now! I was going to get them out of her one way or another.

The wind was crisp as dozens of kids filled the streets in their Halloween costumes. Some scary and some cute. Kids ran by

DEADLY NIGHT

me as if I was invisible. Their mixture of laughter and screams reminded me why I hated this holiday. I hated being scared. I never understood why people enjoyed it so much. Could it be the thought of becoming someone different for the day? Kids taking candy from strangers. Didn't they teach us not to do that growing up? But once a year they allow us to? If we dress up of course. I couldn't imagine living in a big city. Our small town made Halloween a big deal.

I followed far behind Mylah as she walked to the restaurant to meet our mom and Daegan. She was on the phone most of the time. Probably complaining about me. I didn't know if she was talking to her boyfriend or our mom.

In order to get to the main street of our town you had to walk through some woods. On the other side were several businesses. Mylah walked like nothing could bother her. I on the other hand was trembling with fear. My anger is what kept me going. It would have been completely dark if it wasn't for the moon's light shining through the trees in different areas. I tried not to make a sound as I followed her. The laughs and screams became more distant the deeper into the woods we got. Mylah walked along the trail to get to the other side. She was crossing the wooden bridge when she stopped to answer her phone again. I stopped and hid behind a tree so she couldn't see me.

I'm almost there.

She told the person on the other line. I couldn't hear what they were saying to her.

I'm alright.
No, she didn't.
I'm done with her. If she can't accept you then I don't need her in my life.

I understand all that, but we are grown now. I'm old enough to make my own decisions. She likes to be in control of everything but not anymore. This is my life, and I can make my own decisions. If she doesn't like it, she can stay the hell away from me!

I felt the knife go through my heart once again. How could she? I kneeled down and grabbed a thick piece of branch on the ground. I was going to make her regret everything she just said. She was going to regret abandoning me.

I walked at a fast pace to catch up to her on the bridge. I wasn't hiding anymore. She was going to know it was me coming.

Mylah turned around and saw me staring at her with my eyes full of anger. Her eyes widened like a deer in the headlights with her phone still attached to ear. She had nothing to say now. I stood there not saying a word with the thick branch gripped tightly in my hand.

"Breigh," she finally spoke. "Why are you following me?" she took the phone away from her ear finally.

"Why do you think?" I challenged her to answer.

"Look, I love you Breigh, but I just can't live with you anymore." She finally admitted.

"After everything I have done for you?"

"I'm grateful for what you have done. It's time we go our separate ways. I have a whole life that you know nothing about. You don't know who I am anymore."

"I know who you are because I raised you. Not that trash you want to call mom! It was me who made sure you were safe. Who fed you. Who made sure you had everything you needed? Not her! Me!" I yelled at her.

"And your job is done now!" she hollered back. "I forgive her and want her in my life. What don't you understand about that?"

"Why?" I didn't understand how she could forgive her just like that. "She has done nothing!"

"She's a different person than before. She isn't who she once was and all she wants is a second chance. If you don't want to give her that then that's fine. This is my choice and my choice alone. You don't get to tell me what to do anymore."

I felt warm tears streaming down my cold face. I couldn't believe what I was hearing. There was no convincing her otherwise. I was never going to see Mylah again, was I? "You are both trash! You deserve each other!"

"Say what you want about me, but I will not let you speak of my mother that way!"

Hearing her call that woman mother fueled me with even more anger. I swung the branch at Mylah, and she moved back barely missing it. She almost fell backward over the ledge of the bridge, but she steadied herself. She grabbed her chest as she began to hyperventilate. This was my chance to get even with her. I ran to her and pushed her over the ledge.

Mylah screamed loudly before landing hard in the creek. It was only about twenty feet to the ground. I could barely see anything. I listened quietly for breathing sounds. Instead, I heard noises in the distance. Someone was coming. I hid in the trees while a couple walked across the bridge. They acted normally. They didn't seem suspicious of anything. Maybe they didn't hear Mylah scream.

I let out a sigh of relief and made my way back to my apartment without being noticed. Once I was home, I closed the door and locked it behind me. Did I just kill Mylah? I rehearsed in my head what I was going to tell the police when they found her body.

"She was off to meet our mother who abandoned us as children," I would tell them. I was going to put all the blame on her.

My plan would have worked except they never showed up. Her body was never discovered. I waited a couple days to report her missing. I told them she left to go visit our mother and she never returned.

Chapter Fifteen

"You and Daegan set me up? Why am I not shocked by this?" I should have known these two would be up to something.

"We had to." she admitted. "We couldn't let you get away with what you did to Mylah,"

"And all these innocent people had to die tonight?"

"We were supposed to be coming down here alone. Not my fault it didn't work out that way. I didn't like any of them anyways." she said as she rolled her eyes.

"You're right Layla, I did kill Mylah. She tried to leave me like our mother left us. What was I going to do? Sit at home all alone while she forgot about me like our mom did? Daegan was no good for her. Look at the weird stuff he's into. And don't get me started on you."

"What about me?" She looked offended.

"You are the worst of them all. Always around, and not being able to take care of yourself. You kept your hand held out to Mylah and you just used her. You're pathetic and always have been." I let her have it. If she was going to turn me in or kill me, she was going to get every piece of my mind before she did so.

Layla began laughing. "Oh Breigh. The things you don't know." she chuckled.

"What are you talking about?" I asked confused.

"This was more Mylah's scene than ours. She was into the weird stuff. She just hid it well from you." she admitted.

"What are you talking about?" I knew Mylah like the back of my hand. She was your typical girly girl. She couldn't even watch scary movies without getting sick to her stomach.

"Mylah called me that night. After you two had it out about your mom. She told me you were following her. She had a feeling you were going to do something to her. She told me and Daegan plenty of times about the evil streak you would have. Trying to control her."

"Control her? I did everything for her!" I shouted.

"You wouldn't let her breathe. She wanted away from you, and she finally got the chance to when she met Daegan, and you took that away from her. She knew you were going to kill her. This was her last wish for you." she confessed.

"Her last wish for me?" I was heartbroken that my own sister thought those horrible things of me. All I ever tried to do was protect her. I wanted her to be safe.

"Mylah was into some dark stuff, and you didn't even realize it. The butcher and the clown were friends of hers on the dark web. They had no problem trying to take you out for her benefit."

"You are all sick in the head." I told her.

"We wouldn't have had to do this if it wasn't for you." she pointed out.

"You're right Layla. I had no choice but to kill Mylah. And you leave me no choice but to kill you as well."

I ran and tackled Layla to the ground. I sat on top of her and wrapped my hands around her throat. She kicked and tried to scream but I wasn't letting go. She knew my secret and I couldn't let her live to tell another soul. Layla's body stopped jerking and

DEADLY NIGHT

that's when I knew it was safe to let go. I climbed off the top of her and stood above her motionless body.

"If only you knew how to keep your mouth shut." I said to her.

A cough startled me. I turned to see Bryan moving around. "Bryan!" I ran to his side and helped him up.

"What the hell happened?" he asked me distraught.

"I don't know. When I woke up you two were knocked out. I thought you were dead." I told him.

"Is he dead?" he asked looking at Daegan.

"I don't know." I walked over to where Daegan's body was and checked his pulse. I didn't feel anything. I noticed he had a knife partially under him. I grabbed the knife and slid it across his throat. "Well, if he wasn't dead before he is now." I then placed the knife in my back pocket.

"Let's get out of here." Bryan said to me. He had his arm around my neck as I tried to help him walk to the exit door. "Your secret is safe with me." he mumbled under his breath.

I stopped walking. "What did you say?" I wanted to be sure I heard him right.

"Your secret." he repeated. "It's safe with me."

I nodded my head at him and began walking again. I reached into my back pocket and grabbed the knife. I stabbed Bryan in the chest. He looked at me with horror in his eyes when he realized what I had done. I started stabbing him more until he fell to the ground. This time I made sure he wasn't breathing.

I stood over his dead body admiring him. I liked Bryan. I hoped he got out of here and kept his promise to Eugene. He knew my secret and I couldn't let him live. Now I had to find Bella.

I wiped Bryans blood off the knife along with my fingerprints. Then I tossed it next to Layla. I looked at her in disgust. Lying to me for a year. Nobody knew my sister better than I did. Look where lying got her. Dead!

Before walking out the exit door, I grabbed the picture of me and Mylah off the wall and stuck it in my back pocket. The cold breeze stung my face but at the same time it felt great taking that first deep breath. I didn't realize how much I missed the outside world. I survived the night Mylah had planned for me. I bet she was turning in her grave with disappointment.

Chapter Sixteen

One Year Later

It was a crisp afternoon on Halloween. The streets were flooded with kids in costumes as they trick or treated at the local businesses. I sat outside my favorite café once again and read the newest James Patterson book. The story was getting interesting when a middle-aged man approached me.

"How are you doing today miss." he asked me.

I folded a small section of the corner paper so I wouldn't lose the page I was on, closed the book and sat it on the table in front of me.

"I'm doing good sir. What do you want?" I asked him rudely. I was not interested in meeting any new people. Not after what happened last year. I have kept to myself like I always have. It didn't take much to convince the police that Daegan and Layla killed all those people and even tried to kill me. For all they know, they are the ones responsible for Mylah's disappearance.

"I just saw you from across the way and I just had to stop and meet you." he confessed. He had a big grin plastered across his face.

"Look here. I'm not interested in getting to know anyone. So, I suggest you move along." I told the guy as I rolled my eyes at him.

"I'm a nice guy. I think we will be a perfect match." He tried to convince me.

"I don't care if you were the nicest guy on the planet. Get away from me!" I ordered him.

His grin quickly faded. "Wow, you're a major bitch." he blurted out as he walked off angry.

I took that as a compliment and smiled. "I guess we aren't a perfect match." I said under my breath. I picked my book up and continued where I left off.

Not even a minute later a shadow approached me.

"You just can't catch a clue can you." I said without looking up assuming it was the same guy as before.

"Hey Breigh," said a recognizable voice.

I looked up from my book and my jaw dropped. My body clammed up and my heart began to race. I could feel beads of sweat starting to fall from my forehead. I couldn't believe my eyes.

"Mylah!" I said in shock.

Mylah stood there looking at me with a big smile on her face.

Acknowledgements

To my kids for always blessing me with your patience and inspiration. The love you give is one of a kind and it keeps me going. My brown-eyed beauties, nothing will ever compare to you.

To my Frost for always believing in me. For sticking by my side through the success and the failures. My twisted stories haven't scared you away yet and I hope they never do. I love you so much.

To my family and friends for all your support throughout this journey of mine. You are all the best ever.

To my biggest fan, Alyse. Thank you for all the advice and listening to all my rants like you do every book I write. There are so many crazy stories in my head, and you always help pick the next one to be told.

Last but not least, to all my loyal readers. Thank you for taking the time out to read this book along with the others.

Don't miss out!

Visit the website below and you can sign up to receive emails whenever F. A. Witte publishes a new book. There's no charge and no obligation.

https://books2read.com/r/B-A-SOUM-BDXPC

BOOKS 2 READ

Connecting independent readers to independent writers.

Did you love *Deadly Night*? Then you should read *The Bestfriend*[1] by F. A. Witte!

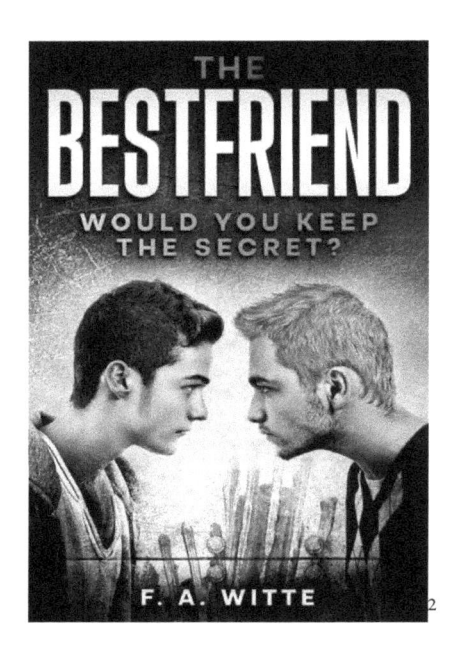

Dalton Baxter and Blake Gibson have been best friends since kindergarten. Now that they have graduated Dalton plans on one day being famous painter while Blake is still undecided.

After leaving a graduation party the duo are in a horrible accident. Dalton would undergo surgery while Blake walks away scratch free.

After being released from the hospital Dalton's girlfriend Morgan Murphy is by his side helping him get better. His

---

1. https://books2read.com/u/3LLwZD

2. https://books2read.com/u/3LLwZD

parents are being strict and forbid him from seeing his best friend but that doesn't stop Dalton from hanging out with Blake.

Blake has a secret and he's spiraling out of control. His near death experience has changed him. When the women he meets are found dead Dalton suspects Blake murdered them. When Dalton confronts Blake he is given a choice. Keep the secret or Morgan is next.

Will Dalton do the right thing or will he do whatever it takes to keep Morgan alive.

Read more at https://fawitte08.wixsite.com/fawitte.

Also by F. A. Witte

Mine
Revenge
The Neighbor
The Fall of Jacintha
The Bestfriend
Deadly Night

Watch for more at https://fawitte08.wixsite.com/fawitte.

About the Author

F. A. Witte was born in Fairview, Oklahoma. She has an associate degree in Medical Assisting. Writing has always been her passion. Starting with poetry, then to short stories, and finally expanding to novels. She has always been a big fan of Poe, King, and Patterson. She likes to get comfortable with a book from any genre when she's not writing, working, or spending time with her family.

Read more at https://fawitte08.wixsite.com/fawitte.

Milton Keynes UK
Ingram Content Group UK Ltd.
UKHW031148311024
450535UK00004B/70